NOODLE
and the
NO BONES DAY

written by *Jonathan Graziano* 🐾 *illustrated by Dan Tavis*

Margaret K. McElderry Books

New York London Toronto Sydney New Delhi

Noodle is a pug.

A silly,

stubborn,

sweet old pug who lives a very busy life.

Some days Noodle likes to go on walks (and see the sights).

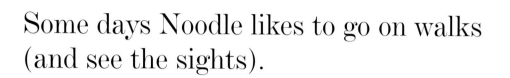

Some days he likes to sit outside (and bark at passersby).

And every day he likes to eat snacks (more chicken, please).

He's a pug
who knows
what he wants.

Jonathan is Noodle's human. He loves taking care of Noodle and joining him in his favorite activities.

He loves to take Noodle on walks (where they can see the sights together).

He loves to sit outside (where they can say hello to their neighbors).

And he loves to share snacks (Noodle prefers chicken but will settle for broccoli).

Jonathan and Noodle do everything together.

One day, Jonathan went to take Noodle on his walk. Noodle lay in his bed with one eye open. He very clearly did *not* want to go on a walk.

"Do you want to see the sights? Or sit outside?
Or have some snacks?" Jonathan asked.
Noodle did not want to see the sights or sit outside.

He did want snacks. But still, he stayed in his bed.

Concerned, Jonathan tried to sit him up.

And Noodle, in his silly, stubborn, sweet way, plopped back down into his bed and went to sleep.

"Wow!" Jonathan said. "It's like he doesn't have bones!"
At that moment, Noodle let out a big sneeze.

(For those who don't speak pug, a sneeze means "yes.")

Huh, thought Jonathan.
Noodle's bones had never
disappeared before.
Was he sick?

Jonathan checked his nose,
but it was soft and perfect as usual.

Maybe Noodle was just sad? Jonathan gave Noodle
a bunch of belly rubs to get him revved up.

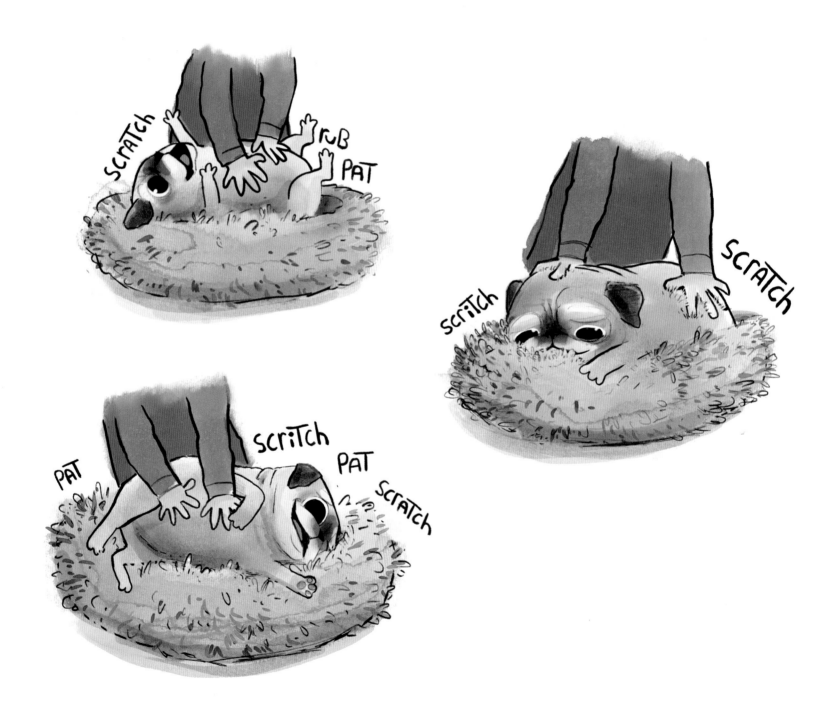

Noodle lapped up the attention, but he burrowed in deeper.

Perhaps Noodle was hungry.

He was, as always. But still, he stayed in bed.

"But what about all of our favorite activities?"
Jonathan asked. Noodle stared at him.

"Would you rather snuggle instead?"
This time, Noodle sneezed.

So that's what Noodle did.

He didn't go on a walk.
He didn't see the sights.
He didn't sit outside.

Instead, he snuggled
in his bed,

he enjoyed lots
of belly rubs,

and he ate
many snacks.

And he was happy.
A happy, silly, stubborn, sweet pug
enjoying a relaxing day—a no bones day!

Jonathan looked at Noodle enjoying his no bones day . . .

and decided he would have a no bones day too!

From then on, some days were bones days—

great days for walks,
seeing the sights,
and sitting outside.

And other days were no bones days—great days for staying in bed, snuggling with a blanket, and getting lots of belly rubs.

(But no matter what kind of day it was, every day was a great day for snacks.)

Bones or no bones,
they are all good days.

To my family, friends, and of course,
Noodle. I'll never know how I got so lucky—J.G.

To my wife, Jessie, who makes every Bones
and No Bones Day that much better.—D. T.

To the snacks I've eaten
and the snacks I've yet to eat.—Noodle

Author's Note

This book wouldn't exist if it weren't for Noodle (obviously) and the millions of
people who have found joy in his sweet personality, glorious flaps, and occasional lack
of bones. I want to thank each and every one of you for your kind words, support,
and genuine love for this sweet king. I adopted Noodle when he was seven
and a half years old, and he's been my best friend for the past six years. All dogs
deserve homes, but I encourage you to check your local animal shelter/rescue next
time you're looking to bring one into your life! Thank you so much!

MARGARET K. McELDERRY BOOKS • An imprint of Simon & Schuster Children's Publishing Division • 1230 Avenue of the Americas, New York, New York 10020 • Text © 2022 by Jonathan Graziano • Illustration © 2022 by Dan Tavis • Book design by Lauren Rille © 2022 by Simon & Schuster, Inc. • All rights reserved, including the right of reproduction in whole or in part in any form. • MARGARET K. McELDERRY BOOKS is a trademark of Simon & Schuster, Inc. • For information about special discounts for bulk purchases, please contact Simon & Schuster Special Sales at 1-866-506-1949 or business@simonandschuster.com. • The Simon & Schuster Speakers Bureau can bring authors to your live event. For more information or to book an event, contact the Simon & Schuster Speakers Bureau at 1-866-248-3049 or visit our website at www.simonspeakers.com. • The text for this book was set in De Vinne. • The illustrations for this book were hand drawn and painted digitally. • Manufactured in China • 0922 SCP • 6 8 10 9 7 5 • CIP data for this book is available from the Library of Congress. • ISBN 9781665927109 • ISBN 9781665927116 (ebook)